the RAVENOUS RAVEN

by **Midji Stephenson**

illustrated by **Steve Gray**

GRAND CANYON CONSERVANCY

Brronk! Craak! Tok-tok-tok!

Raven soars high, flies loop-de-loops, and happily sings, as only a raven can sing. Soon, he gets thirsty and starts looking for a rock pool so he can have a drink.

While drinking, he notices his reflection in the pool. Preening a bit, he thinks, "I am a clever, smart, and handsome bird. Maybe I should eat **MORE** so I can also be a very **LARGE** bird."

So he sets out on a quest for food—
ANY sort of food! He's not picky!
When he spies a Gambel oak, he chortles
with delight. He dives down and scatters
the squirrels because Raven does **NOT**
like to share. When he has the acorns
all to himself, he thwacks,
cracks, and
snacks!

But nuts make him think about
how good fruit tastes with nuts.

Trail mix!

So he goes searching for elderberries.
After scaring some twittering sparrows away, he
picks, slurps, and burps.

With a rumbling belly and a sticky,
purple beak, he heads for the river to wash.
When he sees people fishing, he forgets
about washing and starts wishing for fish.
He spies a whole string of the morning's catch
and thinks, **"Yes! If wishes were fishes..."**
and grabs the whole thing.

Having finished his fish fest, Raven glides over a campsite where a white, oval object catches his eye. "Yes! I love eggs!" thinks Raven as he takes a closer look.

Blech! Pfft! Pfft!

"I think I've been had! This thing's not an egg. It's soap that tastes bad!"

Raven leaves that foul taste behind and goes looking
for a bird's nest because now he **REALLY** wants an
egg—especially one that's more eggy and less...soapy.
Soon, he spots some jay eggs in a pinyon pine, and
with just a few pokes, he has tasty yolks.

After the eggs, Raven considers taking a break,
but then he spies a little gopher snake.
Faster than a monsoon downpour, Raven dives
down and nabs that snake.

With a **wiggle** and a **jiggle** and a small Raven **giggle**, down the gullet it goes.

But snakes make him think about mouse tails,
and mouse tails make him go looking for Coyote.
When he finds Coyote, who is getting ready for a
mouse munch, Raven zips in for a real meal steal.

"Yum!"

Well, mice are tasty but Raven still wants **MORE.** He gets very excited when he sees condors circling overhead because everyone knows what that means.

Dead food ahead!

Even though maggots and dead food
are splendid, he gets side-tracked when
he swoops over some people picnicking
and spots something shiny below.
**"Mmm, a basket open wide!
I wonder what I'll find inside!"**

Someone spots him!

"Eeeeeeeeek!"

He explodes out of the basket
with a bag in his beak.

He flaps to a big rock, and rips opens the bag—
hot dog (plain, no mustard) and chips!
He is, oh, such a hog and wants that hot dog.
And what's this?
Oh, how dandy!
He finds some chocolate candy.

Too full to fly, Raven waddles under a pine tree.
Croaking and gagging, he keels over on his side.
"I really need a nap!"

As the sun sets, he awakens to a chilling sound.
"Please let that **NOT** be a hoot I heard! Great
Horned Owl is a scary bird! This will be a rotten
deal if I become the owl's meal!"

But Raven feels like a fat ball with wings—
flapping and puffing, bobbling and wobbling!
"Lift off now! Oh, help! Oh, please!"
I fear Owl wants what he sees!

Now, months after that close encounter...

Raven is wiser and his black feathers less tight.
He caches food away and sometimes he
even shares with others. While singing his
Raven songs over canyons, deserts, and
forests, he can glide and roll, sail, and soar.
Will he overeat now?

No, nevermore!

Brronk! Craak! Tok-tok-tok!

Frequently Asked Questions

How large is the Common Raven? The Common Raven is the largest bird of the songbird group. An adult bird is 22-27 inches long, has a wingspan of 46-53 inches, and weighs about 2.6 pounds.

How can you tell a raven from a crow? The raven has a larger body, beak, and wingspan than the crow; plus, it has a ruff of shaggy throat feathers. The raven has a wedge-shaped tail and the crow's tail is more fan-shaped. Ravens tend to travel in pairs, while crows are often seen in larger groups.

Can ravens really eat almost anything? As omnivores, ravens CAN and DO eat almost anything—plant or animal—from berries to carrion (dead food). They look for food everywhere—in trees, on the ground, and in garbage cans. Sometimes they cache food (hide it away) for a future snack.

How smart are ravens? Ravens are very brainy birds, having a large brain relative to their body size. They are uncommonly smart and able to learn, remember, and solve problems. These social birds are bold, curious (shiny things do interest them), playful, and often mischievous.

How do ravens communicate? Ravens use a wide variety of calls and beak and wing gestures to communicate. They have been known to mimic other bird and animal sounds, human speech, and even noises around them—a revving motorcycle, a flushing toilet, and more.

Are ravens good fliers? Ravens are the dancers of the sky. They are acrobatic fliers—soaring, gliding, diving, rolling, doing loop-de-loops, and even flying upside down. By alternately flapping and gliding, they can soar to great heights.

Do ravens mate for life? Ravens mate for life and build their nests in large trees, on telephone poles, or on high cliffs. The female raven usually lays three to seven mottled greenish or bluish eggs, which hatch in about three weeks.

Where do ravens live? The adaptable raven is one of the most widespread birds worldwide. They live in a variety of habitats—forests, deserts, scrublands, grasslands, and Arctic tundra. They can be found in wilderness and urban areas. They range across western and northern North America and occur as far south as Central America. Ravens also live in northern Europe, Asia, and even northern Africa.

How long do ravens live? In the wild, ravens have been known to live as long as 17 years. In captivity, some have lived more than 40 years.

Do ravens have any enemies? Ravens have few natural enemies except for humans, large birds of prey, and sometimes coyotes and martens.

Primary sources used: Bernd Heinrich. *Mind of the Raven*, 1999; John Marzluff & Tony Angell. *In the Company of Crows and Ravens*, 2005; Candace Savage. *Bird Brains: The Intelligence of Crows, Ravens, Magpies and Jays*, 1995; and The Cornell Lab of Ornithology online.

This book is dedicated to my sister, Judy Stephenson,
who passed away in 2013. She loved words, birds, and me,
not necessarily in that order.
—M. S.

to C.J. and Gertrude.
—S. G.

Text © 2015 by Midji Stephenson
Illustrations © 2015 by Steve Gray
All rights reserved.

GRAND CANYON
CONSERVANCY

PO Box 399, Grand Canyon, AZ 86023 800/858-2808
grandcanyon.org

Mission Statement
Grand Canyon Conservancy, formerly Grand Canyon Association,
is the official nonprofit partner of Grand Canyon National Park,
raising private funds, operating retail shops within the park, and providing
premier guided educational opportunities about the natural and
cultural history of the region. Our supporters fund projects including trails
and historic building preservation, educational programs for the public,
and the protection of wildlife and their natural habitat.

Composed in the United States of America
Printed in South Korea

Edited by Theresa Howell
Design by David Jenney

Production Date 9.20.18
Plant & Location Printed By We SP Corp, Seoul, Korea
Job / Batch # 82755/WeSP090918

FIRST EDITION 2015

ISBN 978-1-934656-70-9

21   20   19   18   2   3   4   5

Library of Congress Cataloging-in-Publication Data

Stephenson, Midji.
 The ravenous raven / by Midji Stephenson ; illustrated by Steve Gray. — First edition.
   pages cm
Summary: A hungry raven eats everything in sight until he can barely fly. Includes facts
about this uncommonly smart bird.
Includes bibliographical references.
ISBN 978-1-934656-70-9
1. Ravens—Juvenile fiction. [1. Ravens—Fiction.] I. Gray, Steve, 1950– illustrator.
II. Title.
PZ10.3.S833Rav 2015
[E]—dc23
                    2015005301